LOTS OF O'LEARYS
SECONDHAND STAR

MARYANN MACDONALD

ILLUSTRATED BY
EILEEN CHRISTELOW

HYPERION BOOKS FOR CHILDREN
NEW YORK

Text © 1994 by Maryann Macdonald.
Illustrations © 1994 by Eileen Christelow.
All rights reserved.
Printed in the United States of America.
For information address
Hyperion Books for Children,
114 Fifth Avenue, New York, New York 10011.
FIRST EDITION
1   3   5   7   9   10   8   6   4   2

Macdonald, Maryann.
Lots of O'Leary's: Secondhand star/Maryann Macdonald; illustrations by Eileen
Christelow—1st ed.
p.   cm.
Summary: Francie finds life in her large family difficult
sometimes, and getting the dreaded Sister Ursula as her second-grade
teacher does not help, but making a new friend and working on the
class play do.
ISBN 1-56282-616-6 (trade)—ISBN 1-56282-617-4 (lib. bdg.)
1. Catholic schools—Fiction.   2. Schools—Fiction.   3. Plays—
Fiction.   4. Family life—Fiction.]   I. Christelow, Eileen, ill.
II. Title.   III. Title: Lots of O'Leary's: Secondhand star.
PZ7.M1486Se   1994
[Fic]—dc20   93-31812   CIP   AC

The artwork for each picture is prepared using
a pen-and-ink wash. This book is set in 15-point Joanna.

For Megan, who played Dorothy
—M.M.

CHAPTER ONE

"Mom!" yelled Francie. "Jo Jo is eating my notebook!"

Jo Jo, her baby sister, was lying on the floor. She was chewing on Francie's notebook. Jo Jo looked happy. Ernestina, the dog, looked happy, too.

Mom did not come. She was resting. She was going to have another baby.

Francie pulled the notebook away from Jo

Jo. It had teeth marks on it. It had baby slobber on it, too. Francie sighed.

Tomorrow was the first day of school. Francie wanted to start second grade with the right things. She had a new Turtle Twins lunch box. She had new high-top sneakers. But now her new notebook was ruined.

"Thanks a lot, Jo Jo," she said. Jo Jo started to cry. Francie's big sister, Dolores, came in. She picked up Jo Jo.

"Let's sing a song," she said.

They all sang Ernestina's favorite song, "How Much Is That Doggie in the Window?"

"Woof, woof!" went Jo Jo.

"The one with the waggly tail?"

"Woof, woof!" went Ernestina. She wagged her tail.

After the song, Jo Jo crawled off with Ernestina.

"Jo Jo thinks she's a dog," said Francie.

"She's working on her baby teeth,"

Dolores said. Dolores always understood. She was good and she was smart.

Francie asked Dolores, "Would you swap notebooks with me?" Dolores shook her head.

"Ask Ambrose," she said.

Ambrose was in the basement. He was taking apart a broken vacuum cleaner. He was always taking things apart. He didn't ride his bike or play baseball. He took things apart.

Ambrose wiped his glasses on his T-shirt.

Francie asked him for his notebook. "Okay," he said. "It's in my book bag."

So Francie got her brother's book bag. It was brown. It was dull and sturdy, just like Ambrose.

Francie sat down at the kitchen table. She printed "Francie" on her new notebook. She liked that name. It was prettier than her real name, Frances. Dolores looked over Francie's shoulder.

"Second grade is easy," she said, "unless you get Sister Ursula Agnes."

"Who is she?" asked Francie.

"A mean old nun," said Dolores. "She looks like a big black bear. Everyone calls her Sister Grizzly."

Oh no! thought Francie. She had a baby sister who thought she was a dog. She had a big brother who was weird. She had a big sister who was perfect. Could she really get a mean grizzly bear teacher?

CHAPTER TWO

Sister Ursula Agnes sat at the big desk at the front of Francie's class. She was calling the roll. After every name, she looked up over her steel glasses.

"Bonfiglio, Nico." Nicky was blowing a bubble. It popped in his face. The class laughed. "Spit out the gum," said Sister Ursula Agnes. Nicky did.

"Brown, Chiffon."

Chiffon waved her hand from the back. "Here I am."

"Here I am, *Sister*," said Sister Ursula Agnes.

"Here I am, Sister," said Chiffon.

"Carter, Annabelle."

"Present, Sister," said Annabelle. She sat in the front seat. She smiled at Sister Ursula Agnes. Sister Ursula Agnes smiled back.

"O'Leary, Frances."

"Francie, Sister," said Francie. "Not Frances."

"It was Frankie last year," said Nicky.

"It says Frances here," said Sister Ursula Agnes, frowning.

"Frances is my name," Francie explained. "But I like Francie better."

"Hmph," said Sister Ursula Agnes. "Frances is a beautiful name."

"What does she know about beautiful names?" Francie asked Chiffon in the hall.

"Yeah," said Chiffon, "with a name like hers?" She looked at Francie's lunch box. "You still have that old Turtle Twins lunch box?"

Francie nodded. She didn't tell Chiffon it was brand new.

"Girl," said Chiffon, "that's last year's lunch box!" She held up a silver lunch box with pink spacewomen on it. "This year it's Space Sisters," she said. "You've got to get one of these!"

Francie's heart sank. Her lunch box was the wrong kind.

In the playground the class played red rover. Annabelle called the names. She called Chiffon. She called Nicky. She even called Stella Zujak. Stella wore homemade clothes. She ate funny things for lunch. But Annabelle called her before she called Francie.

*　　*　　*

8

When no one else was left, Annabelle said, "Red rover, red rover, let Frances come over!" Francie scraped the gravel with the toe of her shoe.

Annabelle tried again. "Red rover, red rover, let Frankie come over!" Francie looked up at the sky.

"Oh," said Annabelle. "*Excuse* me! Red rover, red rover, let *Francie* come over!" Francie ran across. Annabelle snickered.

"Fancy Francie," she whispered to her friend, "with the stupid sneakers!" She whispered it just loud enough for Francie to hear.

Francie had had enough of second grade. She was ready to go home. But the bell rang.

Sister Grizzly was not in the classroom. Another teacher was there—a young teacher who smiled.

"My name is Miss Walker," she said. "I'm helping Sister Ursula Agnes in the afternoons.

Today we are going to read a story. Do you know *The Wizard of Oz*?"

"I saw it on TV!" said Nicky.

"Me, too," said Chiffon.

Miss Walker smiled. "Did you like it?" she asked.

"It was cool," said Chiffon. Everyone agreed.

"Well," said Miss Walker, "let's see if you like the book as much as you liked the movie."

She began to read. "Dorothy lived in the midst of the great Kansas prairies. . . ."

Miss Walker read for the whole afternoon. She read all about Dorothy's travels in the Land of Oz. She asked the class, "What did you think?"

"I loved the witch," said Chiffon. "She was so bad!"

"The Scarecrow was better," said Nicky. "He was funny."

"It's a good story with good characters," said Miss Walker. "We are going to make it into a great play."

"A play!" Francie said. Miss Walker smiled at her.

"But Miss Walker . . . ," said a voice. It was Sister Ursula Agnes. She was back in the classroom. "My class always does *Saint Francis and the Wolf* for the school show."

"Oh," said Miss Walker. "I'm sorry. I didn't know."

Francie didn't want to do a saint play. She raised her hand.

"Can we take a vote, Miss Walker?" she asked. Miss Walker looked at Sister Ursula Agnes. Sister Ursula Agnes's lips pressed together. But she nodded.

"All right," said Miss Walker, "hands up for *Saint Francis and the Wolf*." Two hands went up. One was Annabelle Carter's. One was Sister Ursula Agnes's.

Then Miss Walker said, "Hands up for *The Wizard of Oz.*" Every other hand went up.

The class cheered. "We'll have tryouts tomorrow," said Miss Walker.

Francie started to walk home alone. But someone called, "Francie, wait up!" It was only Stella Zujak. But Francie waited for her anyway.

"I thought you lived on Bellevue," said Francie.

"I did," said Stella. "Mama and I just moved near you. Now we can walk home together."

Oh goody, thought Francie. She stomped her sneaker in a puddle. Brown water splashed on her socks. She did not care.

"You were brave today," said Stella.

"Thanks," said Francie.

"Are you going to try out for the play?" asked Stella.

"Sure," said Francie. "Aren't you?"

"Yes," said Stella. "I would love to be Dorothy. But I don't think I'll get the part."

"You know who will," said Francie. "Annabelle Carter. She gets everything."

Stella nodded. Annabelle got all A's. She was the prettiest girl in second grade. But she was a show-off and a sneak.

Francie jumped in another puddle, with both feet this time. Water splattered everywhere.

Stella laughed. Francie looked at her. She looked at Stella's long braids and at her homemade dress. Stella looked just like Dorothy. She didn't even need a costume. Except for silver shoes, maybe.

Francie had an idea. She said, "Stella, want to come over to my house?"

CHAPTER THREE

Stella and Francie got oatmeal cookies and milk. They took them up to the room that Francie shared with Dolores and Ambrose. They sat down on Francie's bed. Dolores sat on her bed, reading.

"Now," said Francie, "we are going to practice. Annabelle Carter is not going to be Dorothy. One of us is."

For tomorrow's tryouts, everyone had to

say, "Look out! Here come the Winged Mon-keys!" They had to say it loudly. They had to pretend to be scared. They had to do it in front of everyone.

"Go on," said Francie to Stella.

Stella stood up and brushed cookie crumbs off her skirt. She gulped. "Look out," she whispered. "Here they come."

"That was awful!" said Francie. "Here, watch me." Francie stood up on the bed. She pointed up into the pretend sky. "Look out!" she yelled. "Here come the Winged Monkeys!"

"Francie," Dolores said. "I've got to do my homework in here."

"Oh, all right," said Francie. "Let's go down to the basement."

But Ambrose was in the basement, taking things apart. You could never be alone in Francie's house.

"Don't worry," said Ambrose. "I will not watch."

Stella tried again.

"Louder," said Francie. Stella shouted.

"Good," said Francie. "Now throw your arm out and point. Like this." Stella threw her arm out and pointed.

"Again," said Francie. Stella did it over and over. She did it until her eyes flashed and her braids tossed.

"Pretty good," said Ambrose.

"I thought you weren't watching," said Francie.

"It's better if I do," said Ambrose. "Then you will get used to people watching."

"You are right," said Francie. She called Mom and Dolores and Jo Jo. Ernestina came, too. "Now," she said to Stella, "do it for them."

The first time, Stella's voice was shaky. The second time, she was better. The third time, she was perfect. Mom and Dolores and Ambrose clapped hard. Jo Jo jumped up and down on Mom's lap. And Ernestina barked loudly and wagged her tail.

Stella turned red. "I better go home now, Francie. But thanks for helping me. You are a real friend."

That night Francie sat on her bed and stared out the window. She thought about what Stella had said. She knew she was not a real friend. She had only helped Stella to get even with Annabelle. That rat didn't deserve to be Dorothy. But now Stella was so good she would get the part.

But Francie wanted a part in the play, too! She stared out over the garage roof at the big moon. Then she picked out the biggest star she could see and she whispered,

Star light, star bright,
first star I see tonight,
I wish I may, I wish I might,
have the wish I wish tonight.

"I never wish on stars," said Ambrose. You could not even make a secret wish in Francie's family.

"What do you wish on?" she asked.

"Lightning bugs," said Ambrose.

"That's stupid," said Francie.

"Stars are dead," said Ambrose. "At least lightning bugs are alive. Maybe they can help you get your wish."

"That's the stupidest thing I ever heard," said Francie.

Ambrose went to brush his teeth. Francie went closer to the window. She looked hard for a lightning bug. When she found one, she wished on it—just in case.

CHAPTER FOUR

It was tryout time. Nicky was first. He made his eyes look big. Then came Chiffon. She made her voice high and squeaky. Annabelle Carter was next. She shook with pretend fear.

But when Stella's turn came, she did everything at once. She looked and sounded really scared.,

"All right!" yelled Nicky. Stella blushed.

One by one, all the second graders took their turns.

"Francie?" asked Miss Walker.

Francie stood up. She walked up to the front. She looked out at the faces. She opened her mouth. But nothing came out. Francie's head felt like it was stuffed with straw, just like the Scarecrow's in the story.

"Look out . . . ," Miss Walker whispered.

Then Francie remembered. She raised her arm. She pointed at the door.

"Look out!" she yelled. "Here come the Winged Monkeys!"

Just then, the door opened. Sister Grizzly came in with another nun. Everyone laughed.

"Thank you, Francie," said Miss Walker. "Thank you everyone. Come to the lunch-room after school. We will announce the parts then."

At three, Stella and Francie went to the

lunchroom together. Miss Walker began reading the names.

"The Wicked Witch of the West, Chiffon Brown."

"Way to go, Chiffon," said Nicky. Chiffon's smile stretched all the way across her face.

Miss Walker went on, "Glinda the Good Witch, Annabelle Carter."

Annabelle clapped her hands. "Oooooh!" she cried. "Goody!"

"Goody for a goody-goody," Francie whispered to Stella.

"At least she's not Dorothy," Stella whispered back.

One by one, Miss Walker went down the list: the Scarecrow, the Tin Woodman, the Cowardly Lion, Aunt Em, Uncle Henry, the Wizard of Oz. Then at last she said, "Dorothy, Stella Zujak."

Stella squeezed Francie's hand. "I got it!" she said.

Francie tried to smile. Stella, not Annabelle, was Dorothy. But what was left for her? Miss Walker read out all the Munchkins. She read out all the Winged Monkeys. She did not read Francie's name.

Finally, Miss Walker said, "Toto, Francie O'Leary." She was a dog. Stella put her arm around Francie.

"Congratulations," said a voice behind them. Francie turned to look. It was Annabelle Carter. "Woof, woof," she said.

CHAPTER FIVE

Francie stabbed her meat loaf with her fork. "And then Miss Walker told us all the parts were important," she said.

"Sounds like something a teacher would say," said Ambrose.

"Ambrose," said Dad. He raised his eyebrows. He looked hard at Ambrose. He didn't have to say anything else.

"I think it will be fun to be a dog," said

Mom. Francie looked at Ernestina. She was eating peas off the floor. Ernestina did look happy. But Ernestina was not very smart.

"I will buy some fake fur fabric for your costume," said Mom.

"I will help you sew it," said Dolores.

"I will make you a tail," said Ambrose.

Francie felt better. Her family loved her. They were going to help her even though she was not a star.

"My mom is making me a costume, too," said Stella the next day at play practice. "It's a dress with blue and white checks and a white apron. We're going to dye my old shoes silver." Stella's eyes were shining.

"My whole dress is going to be silver with white net ove it," said Annabelle Carter. "And I'm goi g to wear a golden crown with diamonds."

"Huh?" said Chiffon. "Where are you gonna get that, girl?"

"From Party Time Parade," said Annabelle. "I'm going to have a magic wand, too, with a star on the end."

"I wish I had a magic wand," said Francie. "I would make you disappear."

Annabelle sniffed. "You are all just jealous," she said.

Miss Walker was holding a script. "Today I will read your lines," said Miss Walker. "Say them after me and try to learn them by heart. Now, Dorothy, Toto, Aunt Em, and Uncle Henry . . . onstage!"

Francie got down on all fours. Her part didn't come until Uncle Henry said, "It's a cyclone, Em! Run for cover!" Then she had to crawl fast into a corner. She had to pretend to hide under a bed. When Annabelle came on as the Good Witch, Francie growled at

her. She even snapped at Annabelle's ankles.

At last Miss Walker said, "That's enough for today." Francie stood up. She rubbed her sore knees.

"I knew you would be good as Toto," said Miss Walker. "It's such an important part."

Francie nodded. She knew she was good as Toto. She had learned a lot from Ernestina and Jo Jo. But she also knew being Toto was not that important, no matter what Miss Walker said.

"Frances O'Leary!" a voice said. Francie froze. It was Sister Ursula Agnes. Her arms were crossed on her big chest. "You are just the one I've been looking for," she said.

CHAPTER SIX

"I have something for you," said Sister Ursula Agnes. She handed Francie a fat book. "It's the life story of Saint Francis of Assisi, your patron saint."

"Oh," said Francie.

"He was a very great saint," Sister Ursula Agnes went on. "He wanted all living things to be his sisters and brothers."

I have enough sisters and brothers, Francie thought.

"After you read this you will be proud to be named Frances," said Sister Ursula Agnes.

Francie didn't think so. The book looked boring. It was full of hard words. "I will ask my dad to read it to me," said Francie.

"Excellent," said Sister Ursula Agnes. She smiled at Francie. She looked scary even when she smiled.

Francie slammed into the house through the back door. Her arm hurt from carrying the fat saint book. She dumped it onto the kitchen counter.

"Francie!" Ambrose called. "Is that you? Come and see your costume."

Ambrose, Dolores, Jo Jo, and Ernestina were all in the basement. Ambrose was at his workbench. Dolores was at the sewing

machine. Scraps of fake fur were everywhere. Ernestina was shaking one in her teeth. Jo Jo was copying her.

Dolores held up a big black bag. It had a hole cut in it for Francie's head and four more holes for her legs and arms.

"Like it?" said Dolores.

"This is the tail," said Ambrose. He held up a fur-covered spring. The tail wavered back and forth, up and down.

"Pretty good, don't you think?" said Ambrose.

"What about my arms and legs?" Francie said. "They will look funny sticking out of those holes."

"You can wear my black leotard," said Dolores.

"Well, what am I going to wear on my head?" said Francie.

Ambrose scratched behind his ear. "We will think of something," he said.

"Try it on, Francie," said Dolores.

So Francie tried the costume on. She looked at herself in the long mirror in Mom's room. She looked like a fat cat with skinny legs.

"It's too big," she said. That was the nicest thing she could think of to say.

"Room to grow," said Mom. Mom always said that.

"I don't need room to grow!" yelled Francie. "The play is next Friday." Mom was the only one who would be bigger by next Friday. She was growing fast. "Do you think we could rent a costume from Party Time Parade?" Francie asked.

Mom patted Francie's furry shoulder. "We will see, honey," she said.

"I'm sorry, pumpkin," said Dad after dinner. "Thirty-five dollars is too much money."

"Please, Dad," begged Francie. "Just this once."

"I don't have it, Francie," said Dad. He lifted her onto his lap. "You know I would get it for you if I could."

Francie put her head back on Dad's shoulder. She had not sat on his lap for a long time. Then she remembered the Saint Francis book.

"Daddy," she said, "would you read to me?"

"Sure," said Dad. He gave her a hug.

Francie jumped off Dad's lap. She ran to the kitchen to get The Life of Saint Francis. There it was, on the counter, where she had left it. Only now it was lying in a pool of Kool-Aid.

CHAPTER SEVEN

Sister Ursula Agnes sat behind the big desk. She looked at *The Life of Saint Francis*. Her lips pressed together more tightly than ever.

Francie finished telling her about the Kool-Aid. "My brother Ambrose said we could dry it off in the dryer. But it didn't do any good."

"I can see that," said Sister Ursula Agnes.

"A lot of the pages fell out," Francie went

on. "But most of them are still stuck together. We tried to get them apart with a knife."

Sister Ursula Agnes fingered the torn pages. "Frances, your parents will have to pay for this book," she said.

"I don't think they can," said Francie. "My dad doesn't even have thirty-five dollars to get me a costume for the play. He told me so last night."

"Oh?" said Sister Ursula Agnes. She tapped her fingers on the desk. Then she opened her desk drawer and put the book inside. "I will telephone your mother this afternoon, Frances. Now sit down. I want you to copy 'I must take better care of things' ten times, please."

Francie sat down to write. Second grade couldn't get any worse, she thought. She had to be a dog in the school play. She had to wear a stupid homemade costume. And now she was in trouble with Sister Grizzly.

At play practice, Stella was in trouble, too. She could not remember her lines. Not even in the first act.

"Try just one sentence at a time," said Miss Walker.

Stella was shaking. Everyone was watching her.

"My house must have fallen on the witch," Francie whispered to her.

"My house must have fallen on the witch," Stella said after her.

"Whatever shall we do?" Francie whispered.

"Whatever shall we do?" repeated Stella.

"Good girl, Stella," said Miss Walker. "I knew you could do it."

"I would be dead without you," said Stella on the way home. "How do you remember all that?"

Francie said, "I don't have any lines, so

everyone else's just stick in my head."

"You're lucky," said Stella.

"Don't worry," said Francie. "I'm always onstage with you. If you forget, I'll help you."

Stella hugged Francie. "You are the best friend I've ever had!" she said. Then she ran home.

Francie watched Stella run away. Once she turned and waved at Francie. Francie waved back. Then she put her hands in her pockets. She whistled a soft whistle. Maybe she *was* a good friend after all. Things didn't seem so bad anymore . . . until she got home.

"Francie," called Mom from the kitchen. "I have a surprise for you."

Mom did not sound mad. Maybe Sister Grizzly had not called her.

"Your teacher phoned about an hour ago," Mom said. "She seemed to think you had no costume for the play."

"Oh," said Francie. She crossed her fingers. Maybe Sister Grizzly had forgotten about the library book.

Mom went on, "I told her we were making one for you and that we have everything but the head. So guess what?"

"What?" said Francie.

"She's giving us a head."

"A dog head?" said Francie.

"Well, close," said Mom. "A wolf head. She's sending it home with Ambrose."

"Oh no!" said Francie. "It's from that stupid saint play—she's trying to get even with me!"

"What do you mean?" said Mom. "I think she wants to be helpful."

"I'm not wearing a stupid wolf head," said Francie.

"Why don't you wait and see, honey?" said Mom. "It might be fine."

A giant black head with long ears and fangs

peeked around the corner. "Bowwow," it said. Jo Jo looked at the head and started to cry. Ernestina's ears went down. She slunk behind Jo Jo's high chair.

"Fine?" said Francie. "Do you call that fine?"

Ambrose took off the head. "Whew!" he said. "It's hot in there." He looked at the head. "Maybe we could fold back the ears a little, Francie," he said.

"Maybe we could fold back the fangs, too," said Francie.

"I have to admit it's not my idea of Toto," said Mom.

Jo Jo held up a piece of squished pear to Francie.

"Yuck," said Francie. She didn't want anything from her family. She wanted to be alone. She stomped upstairs. Ernestina followed her.

But Dolores was in the bedroom with

friend. So Francie opened the door to the hall closet. She squeezed in next to the suitcases. Ernestina tried to squeeze in with her.

"Go away, Death Breath," Francie said. But Ernestina's feelings were not hurt. She just licked Francie's face. Francie began to cry.

The wolf head was horrible. But if she didn't wear it, Sister Grizzly would be upset. It was bad enough that all her clothes were hand-me-downs from Dolores. Now even her play costume was a hand-me-down.

"I don't want to be a dog anyway," said Francie to Ernestina. Ernestina's eyes were full of understanding. Francie wiped her tears on her sleeve. She hugged Ernestina. Her mind was made up. She wasn't going to be in the stupid play at all. She would tell Miss Walker tomorrow.

CHAPTER EIGHT

"Look what you have done!" screamed Chiffon. She was playing the Wicked Witch. She was good at it. She began to melt. She waved her arms. She swung her body back and forth. She sank down on her knees.

Stella just stood there watching her.

"You wicked creature," whispered Francie.

"You wicked creature," Stella said flatly.

"Try it once more," said Miss Walker. "Try

to sound really angry. The witch stole your shoe, remember?"

But Stella did not sound very angry. She sounded very tired.

"I'm sorry, Miss Walker," she said. Her face looked red and hot. "I will try to do better next time."

"All right, class," said Miss Walker. "See you here again on Monday. We practice three more times before the play—that's all! So be ready." Everyone left the room but Francie.

She was waiting to talk to Miss Walker alone. She had to tell her that she was not going to play Toto. Miss Walker listened. She did not say anything until Francie was finished. Then she sighed.

"Francie, I want to tell you a story," she said. "Once there was a man who had a store. But he did not like to make poor people pay. So he lost his store. To support his family, the man took other jobs. But he was no good at any of them.

"At last, the man decided to write a children's book. No one wanted to publish it. So he paid to publish it himself. It was a big success. It was called The Wizard of Oz."

"Oh," said Francie.

"Think about it, Francie," said Miss Walker. "Think about why this man was a success."

"Because he didn't give up," said Francie.

"Yes," said Miss Walker. "He tried his best, and he didn't give up."

Francie thought about the horrible wolf head and her ugly costume. She thought about her family, who only wanted to help. She thought about Stella, who needed her. And she made up her mind again.

"All right," she said. "I won't give up."

Miss Walker smiled. Francie smiled, too.

No matter what, I'm going to be the best dog I can be, she decided.

CHAPTER NINE

"I am Oz, the Great and Terrible," boomed Nicky from behind a screen. "Why do you seek me?"

"We have come to claim our promise, O Oz," said Stella.

"What promise?" said Nicky.

Stella bit her lip.

"What promise?" Nicky said again.

"You promised to send me back to Kansas," Francie whispered.

"You promised to send me back to Kansas," Stella said after her.

"Not today," Nicky said. "Come back tomorrow."

Walter Funk roared. He was playing the Cowardly Lion. Francie jumped at the screen. She knocked it down. Nicky fell down, too. Then she jumped up on Nicky and barked in his face.

"Very good, Francie," said Miss Walker. "You, too, Walter and Nicky.

"Stella, try to be quicker with your lines," she said.

Stella did not answer. She just looked down at the floor.

"I do try," Stella told Francie later. "The more I try the more mixed-up I get." Stella was getting worse and worse.

"Want me to come over and practice with you?" Francie asked.

"Not today," Stella said. "I'm so tired. But thanks anyway."

"Don't forget your costume tomorrow," said Francie. "It's dress rehearsal."

The next day, the second grade girls were all in the girls room. They were putting on their costumes for dress rehearsal.

"Check out this cape!" said Chiffon. She spun around. Her shiny black cape twirled around her. Francie put on Dolores's black leotard. She put on the furry suit and her tail. But she left the wolf head in the bag. She was not putting it on until she had to.

Annabelle peeked in the bag. She giggled. "I think Francie has the wrong play," she said. "She thinks she's the wolf in *Little Red Riding Hood*."

Annabelle was wearing her silver dress and

her shiny golden crown. Her hair was fluffed up and she had pink lipstick on. How could someone so mean be so pretty?

Stella asked Francie to button her dress. Francie said, "Stella you have red spots."

"Where?" said Stella.

"Here," said Francie. "They are all over your back." The other girls came to look. Miss Walker looked, too.

"Oh no," she said. "It's chicken pox!"

"Chicken pox!" said Stella.

"Watch out!" said Annabelle. "Chicken pox is catching."

"I had it last year," said Francie. She hugged Stella.

"Oh, Francie," said Stella. "I feel so awful!"

"I guess we can't have a play now at all," said Chiffon sadly.

"Wait a minute!" said Stella. "Francie can play Dorothy. She knows the lines better than I do."

"She does?" said Miss Walker.

"She's helped me all along," said Stella.

Miss Walker looked hopeful. "But if Francie plays Dorothy, who will play Toto?" she said.

"I know!" said Francie. "Ernestina. It would be easy for her to play a dog because she is one."

"I don't think we can have a real dog in the school," said Miss Walker. "There are rules about things like that."

"Well, then," Francie said. "If we can't have a real dog, we can have the next best thing. . . ."

CHAPTER TEN

Francie's family was getting ready for the play. Francie was trying to make her hair stay in braids. Pieces kept sticking out.

Dolores looked perfect. Her shiny hair was tied with a ribbon. She was stuffing Jo Jo into a tiny Toto suit.

"I hope you are right about this, Francie," she said.

"Don't worry," said Francie. "I'm putting her on a leash."

Mom was having trouble with her shoes.

"It's just no use," she said. "My feet are too swollen. I can't get them on." Mom looked like a blown-up balloon.

"Never mind," said Dad. "You will look beautiful in your bedroom slippers."

Beautiful? thought Francie. In those awful old pink slippers? She hoped no one would see them coming in.

But someone did. Sister Grizzly was standing guard right at the school door. Francie saw her staring at Mom's slippers.

But just then, Mom said, "Joe, I think we had better head for the hospital." The baby was coming right now!

"Don't worry about a thing, Mrs. O'Leary," Sister Grizzly said. "We will take good care of the children at the convent tonight." Her terrible smile gave Francie the creeps. And the convent was so spooky! But she couldn't think about it now. The play was about to start!

Dolores and Ambrose went to their seats. Francie carried Jo Jo behind the curtain. Nicky, Annabelle, Walter, Chiffon—everyone was there. Miss Walker was talking to them.

"You will all do fine," she said. "Just remember to keep going, no matter what!"

So Francie did. Even when Chiffon almost flew off the stage. Even when Nicky started laughing and could not stop. Even when Annabelle tripped her and she still had to say to her, "You are as good as you are beautiful." Only a real actress could do that.

"Bravo!" yelled Ambrose at the end. He stood up and clapped hard. Everyone else did, too. The curtain went up and down three times. Francie bowed again and again. She had done it. She had played Dorothy.

"Chiffon, you were the wickedest," said Miss Walker backstage. "Nicky, you were the biggest humbug ever. Walter, I've never seen a lion so brave. Annabelle, we could not have had a more beautiful Glinda."

Then she turned to Francie. "And Francie, you saved the day," she said. She took a bunch of roses and handed them to her. "You were our secondhand star," she said.

Francie smiled and blushed. "Thank you," she said. The sweet smell of the flowers made her feel dizzy. She was going to take them to Stella. She couldn't wait to tell everything to her best friend.

"Frances, get your things," said Sister Grizzly. "We are off to the convent." But Dolores met them at the door.

"Francie!" she said. "Guess what? Mom's had twins—two baby boys. Dad's here now to take us home."

Twins, thought Francie. Two new babies to play with! And she was going home— happy, cluttered, crowded, cozy home! Francie knew just how Dorothy felt when she went back to Kansas. She felt so happy that before she knew it, she reached up and gave Sister Grizzly a big bear hug.

Sister Grizzly looked surprised. Hadn't she ever had a bear hug before? She reached into her deep pocket. She handed Francie an envelope.

"Congratulations, Frances," she said. She took off her glasses. Without them her eyes looked small and sad. She took a handkerchief out of her sleeve. Then she walked off alone down the long hall, shining her glasses.

That night, sitting on her bed, Francie opened the envelope. Inside was a framed picture of Saint Francis. He had a halo. He was walking down a road with a happy wolf. Under the picture it said, "It is in giving that we receive."

"What did you get from that creepy nun?" asked Ambrose.

"She's not so creepy," Francie said. She showed him the picture.

Dolores was looking up names in Mom's baby name book.

"Guess what?" she said. "Ursula means bear. Can you believe that? Sister Grizzly's real name means bear."

"I'm not calling her Sister Grizzly ever again," said Francie. Dolores and Ambrose just looked at each other. But Francie turned away and looked out the window.

The moon hung low, right over the O'Learys' garage. Francie hugged her knees. Tonight, she didn't need wishing stars or lightning bugs. She had just about everything she wanted. Second grade was going to be okay after all.